SANSKRITI

by

Karan More

Sanskriti

Cover design: Karan More

First Edition: 2025

ISBN: 978-93-5592-028-7

Sanskriti

Sanskriti

Disclaimer

This is a work of fiction.

This story draws inspiration from true events and real emotional experiences. Some aspects may reflect reality, while others have been altered or reimagined for narrative purposes.
The intention is to bring the depth of genuine human emotion and lived experience into this fictional story, while still allowing creative freedom in how events unfold.

Names, characters, places, and incidents are either products of the author's imagination or are used fictitiously. Any resemblance to actual persons, living or dead, is purely coincidental.

Medical Disclaimer:

The disease mentioned in this book is real.

However, the medical situations, hospital processes, treatment requirements, and related events described in the story may not fully represent actual real-world medical procedures or protocols.

These details have been adjusted for storytelling purposes.

Readers should not consider the medical descriptions as professional guidance.

For real medical information or advice, please consult a qualified healthcare expert.

Acknowledgment

To my family,
for being my strength through every season of life. Your love, patience, and faith in me carried this story long before the words found their place on paper.

To my friends,
who stood by me with encouragement, honesty, and warmth. Thank you for inspiring me in ways you may never fully realize.

And to you, the reader,
for stepping into this world and giving these characters a home in your heart. Your time, your emotions, and your willingness to feel this journey mean more than I can ever express.

This book exists because of all of you.

"Poverty is like quicksand — once you're caught, it drags you down slowly at first, then all at once. The deeper you sink, the harder it fights to keep you. The only way out is to escape before it takes hold."

— Karan More

Sanskriti

Seated together at the bus stand at 3:30 a.m., they watched the drizzle fall, soft drops echoing on the tin roof. A lone streetlamp flickered above, its light casting restless shadows that swayed with the rain. His hand rested gently over hers, warm against the damp night air. Her eyes shimmered—not with joy, but with the quiet weight of tears she tried to hold back.

Her voice broke as she whispered,

"Do you remember the night you proposed to me? You told me—'No matter what, I won't let anything happen to you. I want to marry you, have children with you, and give you both the best life anyone could dream of.'" Her breath hitched before she spoke again. "We were so young then, so naive. I don't know what we were thinking… I should have known life doesn't always go the way we dream it will."

"How could you have known?" he said softly. "You were just seventeen… life takes time to unfold."

"But you were twenty-four," she murmured, looking down. "You should have known. I don't even know why I said yes—why I ran to you, leaving everything else behind."

He sighed, rubbing his forehead. "We were both young… and in love. No one imagined life would be this hard for us."

"Then why…" her voice wavered, "…why fill me with promises, only to break them? I gave up my nursing admission… my future… all for you."

"You were eighteen when we got married," he replied gently. "You could have said no… you could have run away. But you didn't. We're in this together, always."

They looked at each other in silence. Her lashes could no longer hold the burden of the emotion she carried.

He tightened his grip on her hand. "Everything will be alright, my love. I'll do whatever I can… to make this right."

They sat there, holding each other and crying, as he pressed her head gently against his shoulder.

After a long pause, he finally said, “Let’s go home… it’s too late now.”

With red, sleepless eyes, they rose from the bench and began to walk, their hands still clasped. Each step felt leaden, their silence settling over them thicker than the misty night.

After a few steps, he slipped his hand from hers. “Wait here. I’ll be back in a minute.”

She stopped, her brow furrowing. “Where are you going?” Her voice trembled with disbelief. “Even now… at a time like this… you’re thinking about a cigarette?” Her eyes glistened as she spoke, “Don’t you feel guilty? We don’t even have money for the hospital… and still, you’d spend our last ten rupees on smoke?”

“Shh, shh… darling, I’ll be back,” he murmured, crossing the road toward the cycle-wala to buy a cigarette.

The drizzle had almost stopped when a biker pulled up near the bus stop. He slowed down, eyeing her from head to toe, his smirk widening.

"Arre… itni khoobsurat ho," he said, voice dripping with mockery. "Yeh sab karne ki kya zaroorat thi? Kya mil jaata tumhe? Bolo — kitna logi?"
("You're so beautiful… why do you need to do all this? Tell me — how much will you take?")

Sanskriti froze, too shocked to respond, her breath caught short, leaving her hollow.

"Arre, bolo na," he pressed, leaning closer on his bike. "Pehle mil jaati toh wife bana leta tumhe… ab batao — kitna logi?"

("Come on, say something. If I'd met you earlier, I'd have made you my wife… now tell me — what's your price?")

She just stood there in silence, her mind still struggling to process the words.

"Bolo… das? pandrah?" he taunted. ("What, ten? fifteen?")

She turned away, her face tightening in disgust, and began to walk, ignoring him.

"Madam, twenty? twenty-five? Fine then—forty thousand. Not a rupee more. Let's go, I'll take you right now."

Meanwhile, Nayan returned and caught sight of the scene.

"Oye! What the hell are you saying to her?" he shouted, storming toward the biker.

He grabbed the man by the collar. The biker, startled, struggled in his grip. With a sudden lunge, he bit into Nayan's hand. Pain shot up his arm, forcing him to release.

Before Nayan could recover, the biker shoved him back and sped off into the misty night.

"Arre madarchod! Agar yahan kabhi dikh gaya na… zinda gaad dunga!" he yelled after him. ("You motherf**ker! If I ever see you here again… I'll bury you alive!")

Sanskriti rushed to him, clutching his arm with trembling hands. Tears streamed down her face as she tried to calm him, her own body still shivering from the shock.

After some time, they began walking again, heading home.

On the way, an argument broke out.

"Agar tumhari cigarette ki talab na hoti… toh yeh sab na hota," she said under her breath.

("If you hadn't craved that cigarette... none of this would have happened.")

"Maine kya kiya? Kya maine usse bheja tha?" he shot back.

("What did I do? Did I send him to you?")

He kicked a stone off the road in frustration.

Her lips pressed together, and the rest of the walk passed without a single word.

By the time they reached their building, it was almost 6 a.m.

As they climbed the stairs, a ball came rolling down from the first floor. Chasing after it was Himanshu, their son's friend from the building — just a year older than him.

"Aunty, aunty, please pass me the ball!" he said.

Just then, a door opened and Himanshu's mother called out, "Hey beta, where are you roaming around so early in the morning?"

Sanskriti bent down, brushed her hand gently over Himanshu's head, and tousled his hair. "Such a sweet boy you are... here, take your ball."

"Namaste… how is Aaryan?" his mother asked.

Still serious, Sanskriti replied, "Somehow, by luck, we managed to find the vial today. He's stable for now… but I don't know what tomorrow will bring."

A quietness lingered between them.

"If you need anything, just tell me. Will you have some breakfast?"

"We've already eaten," Sanskriti said. "Right now we just need some sleep."

"Alright… take care."

Sanskriti and Nayan nodded softly and climbed the stairs to their floor.

As she opened the door, the kitchen came into view, partially hidden behind a simple curtain divider in the middle of the single-room house. To the right, just beyond the end of the curtain rod, stood the bathroom door. Beside it, a single bed was neatly placed. On the opposite wall, a cupboard with a mirror stood tall, and next to it a study table and chair—on the chair sat Aaryan's little school bag. Every piece of furniture seemed to quietly narrate the story of a small but warm home shared by a family of three.

They entered, locked the door, and collapsed without even changing.

The next morning, Nayan frowned at the plate before him.

"Yeh kya banaya hai? Isse achha zeher de deti mujhe."

("What have you cooked? Better you give me poison instead.")

Sanskriti snapped back,

"Agar mere paas paise hote toh haan, zaroor de deti… Bina tel aur sabzi ke, yahi hai jo bana sakti hoon."

("If I had the money, maybe I would… Without oil or vegetables, this is all I can make.")

Nayan shoved the dish aside, the steel plate clattering against the floor. Without another word, he stormed out, the door slamming shut behind him.

A few hours later, Nayan walked in, his face heavy."I went to the hospital," he said quietly. "They're asking for twenty thousand more."

Sanskriti looked up. “How is Aaryan?”

“Stable,” he replied. “But the procedure needs that money too… for the vial.”

“And now what?” she asked, her voice flat.

“Now what?” he echoed bitterly.

“You left the job as well…” she said.

“Even if I’d kept working, who would give me a month’s salary in a single day?”

“So leaving the job was the better idea then?”

“Bas… leave it.” He turned away and went into the shower.

When Nayan came out, droplets still clinging to his hair, Sanskriti set a plate of roti and sabzi in front of him.

“Where did you get this from?” he asked.

“Himanshu’s mother gave it to me,” she said.

Nayan said nothing more and began eating, hungry and restless.

“So,” Sanskriti said softly, “have you thought about where we’ll get the money from?”

He looked up at her for a moment, then dropped his gaze and kept eating in silence.

With her eyes growing wet, she let out a quiet plea: 'Say something…"

Nayan finished his food, washed his hands, and walked over to her. He sat on the floor beside the bed, resting his head gently against her chest.

"Darling, I know…" he said softly. "I'm trying to arrange the money. But you know it too, don't you? We've already used every resource—borrowed from everyone we could."

"So now what?" she said, her voice breaking. "We can't just let our son die."

"Did you try reaching out to your parents?"

"I tried," she replied faintly. "But you remember how it went… after we married, they cut all ties with me. Sometimes I wonder if they even know we have a son."

There was a pause. Nayan looked at her intently—into those storm-grey eyes warmed by a faint hue of blue. The sharp lines of her face blended beautifully with her soft, chubby cheeks, giving her a look that was both fierce and tender. Her eyebrows framed her eyes with a natural boldness, making her innocence of eyes even more striking. Her skin was smooth as silk, save for the tiny mark beneath her lips that only made her more unique. And her hair—thick, black, and naturally curvy— framed her like a perfect portrait carved by God in a moment of patience.

Then he said softly, "You know… you look even more beautiful when you're asleep."

Her voice cracked. "Now what? Now what do you want from me?"

"Love," he said simply. "How many times have I told you that?"

"And every time, it comes with some intention behind it," she shot back.

He smiled faintly, unbothered. "But you are beautiful, darling… you know that."

Tears welled in her eyes. "What's the use of beauty," she whispered, "if that beauty can't even save her own child?"

Nayan's eyes lingered on the gold mangalsutra resting against Sanskriti's chest. "We can save one day," he said quietly."

Sanskriti followed his gaze, her fingers instinctively rising to touch the chain around her neck. Her voice thinned.

"But what will this buy us? This small pendant… it won't even cover a day's full cost."

His eyes moved from the mangalsutra to the delicate gold earrings and ring she still wore. He reached out and touched them lightly, his fingertips hesitant.
"All this," he whispered, "will buy us at least two days."

Sanskriti stared at him, her eyes glassy and numb. She wanted to speak, but no words came—only the ache of helplessness filling the silence between them.

Nayan got up and sat beside her on the bed. Without saying a word, he wiped the dampness from her eyes and pressed a quiet kiss to her forehead.

His touch lingered—desperate and fragile—as if holding on to her was the only way he could escape the weight crushing them both. He drew her into his arms, and for a moment the noise of the world—the hospital bills, the empty wallet, the endless fear—fell away.

They held each other in silence, breath meeting breath, the space between them disappearing until only warmth remained. His body met hers, steady at first, then softening. Their lips met—a hesitant touch that carried more sorrow than desire.

It wasn't passion that bound them then, but the ache of two broken people trying to remember what it felt like to be safe.

In that small room, they let exhaustion blur into closeness—a quiet surrender to love, to pain, to survival.

Later, she stood before the mirror on her cupboard, her gaze fixed on the mangalsutra resting against her neck. Her fingers traced the dainty pendant—a symbol of promises that now felt like both a chain and a lifeline.

Behind her, tall Nayan moved quietly, her head aligning perfectly beneath his chin. He slipped his arms around her waist and rested his chin lightly on her shoulder, his eyes meeting hers in the mirror. For a long moment, they simply stared — two reflections bound by love, by despair, and by the fragile thread of hope that the mangalsutra still carried.

Then, Nayan curved an arm around her waist and gently turned her toward him, pulling her a little closer. Their bare feet moved over the cold floor as they swayed softly to an unseen rhythm, humming their own mixed version of the song.

"Mera tujhse tha pehle ka naata koi... Yunhi nahi dil lubhata koi..."

Sanskriti smiled and looped her hands around his neck. Their eyes locked, and as she joined in, her voice melted into his—together, they slipped into the melody.

"Mera tujhse tha pehle ka naata koi... Yunhi nahi dil lubhata koi..."

"Teri paheli pe main paheli hoon jo... Na koi samjhe sanam, yeh rishta hai woh..."

"Samundar toh bas sirf ek kadam... Aajaaun tere sang uss chaand tak jo..."

"Mera tujhse tha pehle ka naata koi... Mehsus karaiye janmon ka saath wahi..."

La la la... la la la laa...

"Dil ke taaron se likhi yeh dastaan, Tu hai meri rooh, main tera aastha..."

"Kismat ne likhi kahaani hai jo... Aankh bandh kare janmon tak nibhaani hai woh..."

"Mera tujhse tha pehle ka naata koi... Ek duje bagair yeh maya nahi..."

"La la la la... la la lalla..."

English translation

"There was a bond between us long before we ever met...
Hearts don't get drawn to someone without a reason..."

Sanskriti smiled and looped her hands around his neck. Their eyes locked, and as she joined in, her voice melted into his—together, they slipped into the melody.

"There was a bond between us long before we ever met...

Hearts don't get drawn to someone without a reason..."

"I am the riddle within your riddle—
a love so strange, no one could ever truly understand..."

"The ocean is only a single step away...
Come, let me walk beside you all the way to the moon..."

"There was a bond between us long before we ever met...
Let us feel the togetherness of countless lifetimes..."

La la la... la la la laa...

"This story is written with the strings of our hearts;
you are my soul, and I am your faith..."

"A tale written by destiny itself—
a vow to be kept, even with eyes closed, for lifetimes to come..."

"There was a bond between us long before we ever met...
Without each other, this world has no meaning..."

"La la la la... la la lalla..."

Later, Sanskriti unclasped her mangalsutra. As she placed it in Nayan's hand, she looked at it one last time, her voice low and distant.

"That man offered fifty thousand… for something we've done a thousand times." she said with a hollow laugh, her eyes still fixed on the gold pendant resting in her palm. "Do people really have that kind of money—to waste in one night, while we're here begging to save our son?"

The room fell silent. Even the ticking clock sounded too loud. Nayan looked at her, unsure whether the pain in her words came from anger, shame, or exhaustion.

"Paise bhi kya cheez hai…" he murmured. "Jisko zarurat hoti hai uske paas nahi, aur jiske paas hota hai, usko ahmiyat pata nahi."

("Money… what a strange thing. Those who truly need it never have it, and those who do never understand its worth.")

Sanskriti stared at him for a moment, then slowly gathered her mangalsutra, earrings, and ring into her palm. Without a word, she held them out to Nayan.

He took them hesitantly, his eyes heavy with guilt. Then, taking a thin piece of black thread, he tied it gently around her neck, letting it rest where the mangalsutra once was.

For a long moment, neither of them spoke. The fragile thread swayed softly against her skin—plain, ordinary, yet carrying the same promise that gold once did.

Nayan sold the jewelry and met Sanskriti outside the hospital.

"How much did they give?" she asked.

"Fifty five thousand," he replied, handing over the bundle of notes to her.

Together, they went inside and paid □35,000 at the reception—□15,000 for the periodic vial, a part for daily medicines and pending fees, and another □5,000 as an advance for the upcoming treatments.

Then they walked toward the ICU.

Through the glass, they saw their son lying utterly still, the ventilator breathing for him. The rhythmic beeping of the monitor filled the corridor. Nayan and Sanskriti stood side by side, tears slipping down their cheeks in silence. Sanskriti folded her hands, murmuring a shaky prayer under her breath.

When they finally stepped out of the hospital, Nayan stopped near the gate.

"Sanskriti… give me a little money," he said quietly.

She looked at him, wary. "For what?"

"Just a hundred and fifty rupees."

"Why? What for?"

"Just give it to me, please."

Her tone hardened. "No. You're not going to drink again."

"Baby, come on…" he said, his voice turning soft, almost pleading. "We've got enough to manage for a day or two. Just for today, please."

She hesitated, torn between anger and pity, but before she could turn away, Nayan snatched the money from her hand.

Sanskriti's eyes filled again—not just with tears, but with a kind of exhaustion that words could no longer hold.

As Sanskriti walked back home, she saw her landlord — Megha, a distant relative — standing in the gallery passage near their door.

"Sanskriti," Megha said firmly, "please give me the rent."

"Megha… I know it's improper to ask, especially when I already owe you so much," Sanskriti replied, her voice low. "But please, could you give me one more month?"

Megha sighed. "Sanskriti, it's already been six months. The pending rent has even crossed your deposit amount. Please try to understand, I need the money now. I've never once come here to ask for rent before, but this time… either pay it or leave the place."

Sanskriti stood silent for a moment, then opened her purse with shaking hands. "I only have ten thousand right now," she said quietly. "I can give you that."

"At least give me two months' rent," Megha insisted. "I really need it."

Sanskriti hesitated, then pulled out another five thousand rupees. "Please… take it," she said, her voice breaking as she handed the money over. Her eyes glistened with shame.

Just then, Nayan appeared at the end of the passage.

Megha's tone turned bitter. "See? He always has money for his drink, but not for rent — not even for his child's medicines."

Nayan froze. His face went stiff, his jaw tightening. He wanted to respond, but the words never came. Powerless and ashamed, he stood there in silence as a few neighbors watched from their doorways — quiet spectators to his humiliation.

When they returned home, neither had anything left to say. Whatever money they had was gone, and with only five thousand left from the gold they had sold, they still had to find a way to survive tomorrow.

That night, they went to bed on empty stomachs.

Sometime after midnight, Nayan stirred. He rose quietly and slipped out of the house. Sanskriti saw him leave but was too weak, too drained, to ask where he was going.

A while later, her phone rang. The screen showed an unknown number. Her heart pounded. With unsteady hands, she answered, praying it wasn't from the hospital.

And it wasn't.

It was from the police station.

A familiar voice came through the line, asking her to come immediately. Shocked and confused, Sanskriti rushed out into the night.

At the station, she learned that Nayan had tried to rob the same gold shop where they had sold her jewelry earlier that day.

"Thank God we caught him during our patrolling, before he could break the shutter," said the havaldar, shaking his head.

Through the half-open door, Sanskriti saw Nayan sitting on the floor — a dark, swollen mark on his cheek and a red welt from a police stick across his hand.

Folding her hands, her voice trembling, she said, "Thank you, Bhau. I beg forgiveness on his behalf."

"Nako, nako, vahini," the havaldar replied gently. "Kashala trass gheta tumhi?

(No, no, sister-in-law. Why take so much trouble?)

I know what you're going through. I've told my senior officers everything — how your son's operation can only be done at Kare Hospital. Don't worry, your husband won't be put in jail."

"Thank you so much, Bhau," Sanskriti said, tears in her eyes. "You've saved us from even greater trouble. He did it out of desperation… please forgive him this once."

"Don't thank me, vahini," the havaldar said, lowering his voice. "Just see if you can manage something for the senior officers. I don't want anything, but we need to make them understand."

Sanskriti hesitated. "Will one thousand be enough?" she asked.

The havaldar glanced at her worn purse and spoke softly, "They're asking for fifteen. You try five — I'll tell them to adjust."

With no choice left, desperate to free Nayan, Sanskriti handed over what little they had left.

As they were leaving, the havaldar raised his voice behind them.

"Ye kai re, parat nako karus ase disla na tar saral att takin!"

("If you ever try something like this again, I'll thrash you straight away!")

With a scoff under his breath, he added, "Baiko evdī pāya padte tujhya sāṭhī, ani hā dāru pīun chori karto..."

("Your wife falls at people's feet for you, and you go stealing after drinking...")

Later, as dawn crept in, the two of them walked out of the police station side by side — silent, exhausted, stripped of almost everything they had left.

On their way back home, they passed by the hospital where their son was admitted. Sanskriti stopped for a moment, folded her hands, and prayed silently for his recovery.

A few steps ahead, they reached the same bus stop from the previous night. Under the dim streetlight, a group of women stood in a line — waiting for customers.

Sanskriti looked at them, her voice wavering as she said,

"Instead of all this… maybe it would've been better if I'd sold my body for money. What would I have done alone if you'd been put in jail today?"

Nayan froze in his tracks. His face twisted with pain as tears welled in his eyes. Then, suddenly, he began hitting himself — slapping his own face again and again. The sharp sounds echoed through the empty street. People turned to stare, but he didn't stop.

Through his sobs he kept murmuring, "What have I done… what have I done? I can't even take care of my own child. My son is lying in a hospital, and I'm here — drunk, useless, with no money… I failed as a father."

Sanskriti wanted to console him, but she was too depleted, too angry to think for him this time. She didn't stop. She simply kept walking — leaving Nayan behind, a broken man crying in the middle of the road.

✧ ✦ ✧

Later that night, they sat awake, searching for a way to arrange money for the next day.

By morning, every option had run dry. With no close relatives left to turn to, and every friend and favor already exhausted, there was no one else to ask.

That evening, around 8 p.m., Nayan came home after another long day of searching. His shoulders sagged, his face dull with defeat.

So… did you find anything?" Sanskriti asked softly.

He shook his head. "No. Even if we both worked the whole day, no one would pay us five thousand — forget twenty."

Sanskriti noticed a small keypad phone slipping out of Nayan's pocket.

"What's that?" she asked.

Nayan gave a crooked smirk. "Forget it. I tried selling my smartphone for this one… but I barely got fifteen hundred rupees."

Her eyes dropped to his wrist — the golden watch was missing.

“And where is your watch?” she asked softly.

He looked away. “Sold it. Seven hundred.”

Sanskriti gently caught his hands, her chest tightening with pity and helplessness.

“That watch… it was the last thing you had of your father.”

“Right now, nothing matters more than my child,” he replied quietly.

“But Nayan…” her voice broke, “these small amounts won’t even make a dent. And you’re giving up the pieces that matter the most to you. ”The heaviness in her heart grew — not because of the money, but because of what he was sacrificing.

After a long pause, she added quietly “I went to the hospital today,” she said quietly. “Somehow, I convinced them to give us one more day to arrange the money.”

A growing tension pushed through her voice. “What will we do, Nayan? How will we survive this?”

“There is… one option,” he said slowly. “But I don’t even want to say it out loud.”

Her voice shook, her emotions taking a wild hit as she snapped. "No, Nayan. How could you even think of something like that? How can such a thought even find a place in your mind? I would rather die than do something so shameful."

"Then what should I say, haan? What am I supposed to do — watch our child die?" His voice cracked as he went on. "I love him, Sanskriti… I love him."

He paused, lowering his head. "You were the one who said that man offered us so much money — for something we've already done a thousand times. I'm only saying… just once. Just until we're stable. You'll be safe, we'll be careful, and then… we'll forget it ever happened."

Before he could finish, Sanskriti's hand struck his face. The sound echoed through the room.

She turned away, her breath shaking, tears spilling uncontrollably. Rushing into the bathroom, she locked the door behind her. Inside, her muffled sobs filled the silence that Nayan was too broken to interrupt.

An hour later, Sanskriti stepped out of the bathroom.

Nayan looked at her; she met his gaze, her eyes hollow from crying.

"I'm sorry," he whispered. "But do you have any other plan?"

Sanskriti stared for a long moment, then gave a slow, defeated shake of her head.

He placed his hands gently on her shoulders, his voice breaking. "We'll get through this. Somehow."

In silence, she walked to the cupboard and pulled out the red sari he had given her on their anniversary. The fabric slipped through her fingers, heavy with memory.

"Promise me…" she said faintly. "Once our son gets better, this will be forgotten. From tomorrow, we'll start again. We won't repeat this, and we won't depend on this."

"I promise," Nayan said quietly.

She nodded once. The room felt smaller, heavy with the weight of what they were about to lose — not just dignity, but the last fragile pieces of peace between them.

Both of them left the house and walked toward the bus stop in silence. The night air felt heavier than usual; even the streetlights seemed dim.

"You stay near the women waiting there," Nayan said quietly. "I'll stand on the other side."

"No... I'll be uncomfortable," Sanskriti replied. "Just turn away. If I feel unsafe, I'll call out."

He hesitated, then nodded silently, knowing there was no other option left. He crossed to the other side of the road, facing away from her.

As decided, Sanskriti walked toward the bus stop and stood beside the other women. Almost instantly, every passing biker slowed down, their eyes lingering on her.

Each time someone approached, she instinctively stepped back. When a man came closer, her words stumbled, her gaze flicking to the other side — where her husband stood, unable to meet eyes. And each time, she stepped back again.

After a while, one of the women looked at her with a teasing smile.

"What happened, nayi hai kya?" ("What's wrong — first time here?")

Sanskriti said nothing. Her eyes remained fixed on Nayan.

"Arey ladki, bolegi?" the woman pressed, glancing at him. "Kya tere pati ki koi fantasy–shantasy hai kya?"

("Hey girl, will you speak or not? What, does your husband have some kind of fantasy or what?")

Sanskriti lowered her gaze, silent.

"Sun," the woman said, half-smiling, "agar aise hi sharmayegi na, toh khali haath reh jayegi. Dekh mujhe."

("Listen, if you keep being this shy, you'll go home empty-handed. Watch me.")

A man got off his bike and began walking toward Sanskriti, but before he could reach her, the other woman stepped forward and led him away toward a narrow lane behind the road.

Sanskriti watched as they disappeared into the shadows.

Moments later, another car slowed to a stop near the curb. A man stepped out and began to approach her. Sanskriti's breath grew uneven, but this time she didn't step back.

He spoke — words blurred by the pounding in her ears. His tone was casual, transactional.

"Arey, bolegi kitna?" ("Hey, will you say how much?")

Only a faint, shaky whisper escaped her throat — a number that broke apart mid-air.

"Pa… paa… pachaas hazaar…" ("Fifty… fifty thousand rupees.")

The other girls burst into laughter. One of them smirked.

"Kya… virgin hai kya?"

("What, are you a virgin or what?")

Their laughter echoed under the flickering.

The man sneered. "Paanch hazaar dunga." ("I'll give five thousand.")

He stared at her for a long moment, and she gave a slow nod — a faint sound escaping her lips, barely a word, but enough. The world around her dimmed — the laughter faded, the lights blurred — and all she could hear was the rush of blood in her ears, echoing the weight of what she had just spoken.

They began walking down a narrow path behind the highway.

The man approached her, his steps unsteady. Sanskriti trembled as he drew closer. The sharp stench of alcohol hit her like a wave.

And then — a police siren tore through the night.

In seconds, chaos erupted. People scattered in every direction, like ants crushed under a careless foot. Sanskriti froze. Her mind went blank; her legs felt glued to the ground. She couldn't move, couldn't think.

Then, a hand grabbed hers — firm, urgent. She was yanked into the shadows beside an old, crumbling building.

A woman's voice hissed in the dark. "Tu kya navi hai kya?" ("You new here or what?")

Sanskriti nodded faintly.

"Kitna?" the woman asked.

Sanskriti blinked, confused.

"Arey… kitna maanga tha usne?" ("How much did he offer you?")

"Paanch," Sanskriti whispered. ("Five.")

The woman looked her up and down, then scoffed. "Tu pagal hai kya? Are you nuts?"

Sanskriti said nothing.

"Main tujhe pandrah dilwaungi," the woman said, smirking. "Lekin upar ke mere."

("I'll get you fifteen — but my cut comes first.")

Sanskriti nodded hesitantly.

"Aur pehle wale se paise nahi liya tha na?" ("And you didn't take money from the first one, right?")

Sanskriti blinked. "Aapko kaise pata?" ("How do you know?")

The woman laughed, a short, bitter laugh. "Agar usne paise diye hote na, to tujhe leke bhaagta. Waise bhi, woh chirkut fukat mein hi aaya tha." ("If he'd actually paid, he would've dragged you off. Anyway, that cheap bastard was here for free.")

She straightened her dupatta and jerked her head for Sanskriti to follow.

"Chal mere saath. Aur yaad rakh — hamesha paise pehle, thukai baad mein."

(“Come with me. And remember — money first, the rest later.”)

They walked down the dark path between the bushes. The woman glanced over her shoulder, looking back as Sanskriti followed her.

“Hey — mera naam Rose hai. Red Rose.” She gave a crooked smile. “Tera naam kya hai?” (“What’s your name?”)

Sanskriti hesitated, her gaze flicking to Rose’s blond hair. In a small, stuttering whisper, she managed, “Shh… Sanskriti.”

Rose smiled faintly — a strange, almost protective softness in her tone.

“Sab samajhna padega tujhe… aaj se tera naam Mallika.”

(“You’ll have to learn how things work here… from today, your name is Mallika.”)

As she slid a thin branch away from her face while walking down the narrow path, Sanskriti’s eyebrows lifted slightly. Innocence still lingered in her eyes as she repeated the name softly to herself — Mallika.

Then Rose led her to the back of an old building, where darkness seemed to swallow everything. The trees stood bare, their fallen leaves scattered across the ground. The soil had turned to wet mud from the rain, and each step they took made a soft splash. The air was thick with the damp, heavy smell of decomposed leaves.

Sanskriti saw a car in the distance, its parking lights blinking. As she moved closer, more cars emerged from the shadows — each with a woman standing beside it.

A man laughed from somewhere across the road — playful, mocking.

“Aah Rose… meri Red Rose! Kisko saath leke aa rahi hai tu abhi?”

(“Ah, Rose… my Red Rose! Who are you bringing with you now?”)

Rose shot back without hesitation.

“Navi member aayi hai — just fresh. Bol, kitna dega?”

(“A new one’s here — fresh. Tell me, how much will you pay?”)

“Twenty,” he said lazily.

Rose snapped. “Ja, tu udhar Jasmine ke paas ja. Usko sunghne — tere se nahi hoga.”

(“Go sniff around Jasmine instead… you can’t handle this one.”)

He laughed again.

“You’ve got quite a mouth these days, Rose. Say your final price.”

“Forty.”

“Thirty, final. She’s new — and pretty. I’m being generous. Otherwise, fifteen would’ve done.”

Rose scoffed and pushed Sanskriti gently toward him.

“Ja… mazza kar. Main yahin hoon.” (“Go on… enjoy yourself. I’m right here.”)

The man’s eyes raked over her.

“Naam kya hai tera?” (“What’s your name?”)

“Mmm… Mallika,” she whispered.

“Get in the car,” the man said.

He handed the money to Rose without looking away, then opened the car door and got inside. The door shut behind them with a dull thud that seemed to echo far too long.

A while later, Nayan came searching. From a distance, he saw the faint outline of a car — a saree's pallu caught in the door, fluttering in the breeze. The pattern was familiar — the same saree he had helped Sanskriti drape that morning.

For a moment, his mind refused to understand. Then realization struck — and the world went still. His breath caught, his vision blurred, and without thinking, he turned and ran. Not toward her, but away — because facing it would have broken him completely.

Rose watched him disappear into the night, her face unreadable, before turning back to the car.

A few minutes later, the man stepped out, adjusting his shirt.

"Bring her again tomorrow," the man said, "and I won't pay this much next time."

Sanskriti followed, her steps dragging through the mud. The night felt heavy, the world distant. Shame clung to her like her own skin. Her throat ached, her breath shallow, her eyes refusing to rise.

Rose handed her a bundle of notes.

"Ye le... gin le. Jaise wada kiya tha, pandrah."
("Here — count it. Fifteen, just like I promised.")

Sanskriti took it silently, her fingers trembling.

Rose's tone softened.

"Shayad tera mard yaha aaya tha tujhe dhoondne... aur rote-rote chala gaya."
("Maybe your husband came looking for you... and left in tears.")

The words struck like a blade. Sanskriti froze. Tears welled, blurring everything.

Rose slipped a small, folded slip of paper into her blouse.

"Call this number tomorrow," Rose said.

Without another word, Sanskriti turned and ran — whether to find her husband, or to flee the night itself, even she didn't know.

Sanskriti reached home. Nayan was there, lying still, pretending to be asleep.

She entered quietly, her footsteps barely making a sound. Without a word, she went to the bathroom, took a long shower — as if to wash away the night — and dropped her clothes into the bucket to wash.

When she returned, she slipped into their single bed. Nayan was already lying on the floor beside it.

They both faced away from each other — silent, restless, sleepless. Neither could bring themselves to speak, nor find the courage to meet the other's eyes.

By 4 a.m., neither of them had slept. The room held its breath with them, soaked in silence. Sanskriti heard Nayan stir; a moment later he got up quietly and left the house. She didn't utter a word.

When Sanskriti finally opened her eyes, it was 10 in the morning. Nayan was lying on the floor, reeking of alcohol, passed out in a different shirt.

She washed up, cooked a simple meal, and left it on the table for him before heading to the hospital.

At the hospital, she checked on her son. He was stable—but the bills were not. She deposited fifteen thousand for the previous day's pending amount, yet the dues for the current day were still left. As she stood behind the ICU's glass wall, watching him fight for his life, the nurse's words replayed in her head: they needed money that very day, □25,000 for the next morning's injections only, and □1,25,000 for the surgery scheduled in three days.

The weight of it all pressed against her chest like a stone.

When she returned home, nothing had changed. Nayan was still on the floor, the food untouched, the house quiet. She sat down, tears spilling silently, and whispered a broken prayer.

"Hey God, please… take me away from this. Just finish it."

Hours passed before Nayan finally woke up — his face pale, eyes heavy with a brutal hangover. He avoided her gaze.

Sanskriti gathered the last bits of courage she had, poured a glass of water, and handed it to him. He drank slowly while she sat beside him, her hands were cold; her heart, tired. She held his hand gently.

Sanskriti's voice was soft, almost breaking. "Nayan… I know this must have been hard for you.

But just imagine how hard it's been for me to handle everything. You said you'd be with me in this… Please, don't make it harder by drinking and giving up."

Nayan didn't say a word at first. He got up, splashed water on his face, and returned. His voice was hoarse from the night before as he spoke.

"I'm sorry… I drank too much. I made it worse for you. I won't drink now."

Sanskriti quietly offered him the food.

After a pause, he asked softly, "Have you eaten?"

Sanskriti didn't reply. She just sat there, staring at the plate between them. He asked her again to eat with him, and this time, she quietly joined.

As they sat together, she told him everything the doctor had said about the required amount. After a long silence, they both agreed to continue like this for a few more days — until they found a stable source of income.

✧ ✦ ✧

Later that night, Sanskriti stepped out and called Rose. Her voice wavered as she said she needed more money.

"Aa… par is waqt jagah alag hogi," Rose replied calmly.

("Come… but this time the location will be different.")

When Sanskriti arrived, Rose was waiting near the corner of the street. Neither spoke. Sanskriti followed her through the quiet, narrow lanes between the bungalows until they stopped before one.

The house rose before her like something out of another world — lavish and unreal. Warm golden light spilled through tall glass windows. It glinted on the polished marble steps and on brass handles that gleamed like gold. The air smelled faintly of wet soil and luxury. Expensive cars lined the driveway, their glossy surfaces reflecting the night like black mirrors.

Sanskriti froze. The glow of the place almost mocked the darkness she had just walked through. It was beautiful, yes — but cold. Like a palace built for someone else's story, not hers.

"Yeh client location hai," Rose said, her tone steady. "Idhar zyada milega. Tere jaisi navi ladkiyon ki hamesha demand hoti hai."

("This is a client's place. You'll earn more here. There's always demand for new girls like you.")

Sanskriti didn't answer, but her silence was its own kind of surrender. She followed Rose inside.

The night passed slowly — like a wound being carved without sound.

When she returned home at 4:00 a.m., her fingers clutched □50,000. Enough to clear the hospital's dues. But she knew, deep inside, this was only the beginning. She would need more — much more.

As she reached home, the house was empty. Nayan wasn't there. A flicker of worry rose in her chest, followed quickly by a strange relief — at least she wouldn't have to face him right away.

She moved through the room in silence, just as she had the night before. She dropped her clothes into the bucket, turned on the shower, and stood beneath the cold stream, as if she could wash away something that had sunk too deep to ever leave.

When she stepped out, there was a knock at the door.

Nayan stood there — swaying, drunk, his breath thick with alcohol. Without a word, he stumbled inside and lay on the floor, turning his back to her.

"Why are you drinking so much?" Sanskriti asked softly.

He didn't respond.

She tried again, louder this time. "Tell me! Why are you drinking so much? And where are you even getting the money for this now?"

He turned slightly, his eyes bloodshot. "At least I'm not taking your veshya money," he muttered bitterly.

The words cut deeper than any slap. For a moment, everything inside her cracked. She stepped forward and struck him twice across the face — not out of rage, but out of pain.

"Don't you dare call it that," she choked out, her voice trembling. "I'm doing this for our son — for your son."

Tears blurred her vision as she ran out into the corridor, her sobs echoing through the dim passage.

When she finally returned, he was already asleep on the floor, his face turned away. Sanskriti stood there for a long time in the half-darkness — exhausted, hollow — and then quietly lay down, too.

The silence between them that night wasn't ordinary. It was the kind that builds walls — the kind that doesn't need words to hurt.

The next morning, after waking up, the silence between them lingered like a shadow.

Sanskriti broke it first. "What was that?" she asked quietly.

Nayan looked up, confused. "What?"

"What you said yesterday," she said, her voice tightening. "You know we both agreed to this. I didn't choose this alone—or out of my own will."

Nayan lowered his gaze. "I'm sorry, Sanskriti," he murmured. "It's just… right now I feel worthless. I'm broken by my own thoughts. I can't even provide for my family. And watching you go through this because of me… it's killing me inside."

"So what then?" she asked, her tone rising. "You'll just keep drinking? Keep throwing these words at me? Do you even know what I'm going through? Do you see me drinking?"

She leaned forward, her voice wavering now. "For God's sake, Nayan… for our child's sake. Please don't drink. That's the one thing you can still control."

He looked at her, eyes tired but sincere. "I'll remember that," he said quietly.

She extended her hand toward him. "Promise me."

Nayan reached out and took her hand, gripping it tightly, as if anchoring himself to what was left of them.

"I promise," he said.

Days passed as Sanskriti struggled between attending clients and managing the hospital bills, always trying to catch up. Then one afternoon, Rose called earlier than usual.

Sanskriti frowned as she answered. "Why did you call? I told you not to, unless I call first."

Rose's teasing voice came through the line. "Kya tu bhi, Mallika baby… Jaldi aa ja RM Road ke parlour ke paas. Tera makeover karna hai." (Come on, Mallika baby… hurry to the parlour on RM Road. We're doing your makeover.)

"Makeover?" Sanskriti asked, confused.

"Tu aana… main sab samjhaungi," Rose said with a laugh. (Just come, I'll explain everything.)

Sanskriti sighed. "Fine. I'll come."

When she reached, Rose was waiting at the corner of the street, a cigarette in hand and mischief in her eyes.

"Why did you call me here? And what makeover?" Sanskriti asked.

"Client, Mallika baby," Rose said, grinning. "For them, we have to look the part."

"I don't want to keep doing this for long," Sanskriti muttered.

"Haan, but this is how you earn better, baby," Rose said lightly, looping her arm through Sanskriti's. "Now come on."

She dragged her into a lavish parlour where everything gleamed under warm, honey-colored lights. Sanskriti had never been to such a place before. The attendants made her sit before a tall mirror that reflected a woman she barely recognized.

Haircut, hair wash, colouring, manicure, pedicure, waxing — Rose ordered all of it for both of them.

Rose clapped her hands. "Wah baby… you're looking like a doll now."

Then she turned to the cashier. "Bill batao."

"Twenty-five thousand," came the reply.

Rose turned to Sanskriti with a sly smile. "Pay up."

"What? But I don't have money for this!" Sanskriti's voice cracked.

"Kal hi to di thi na," Rose said, snatching her purse. "Main le leti hoon."

(I gave it to you yesterday… I'll just take it.)

She pulled out □25,000 and handed it to the counter before Sanskriti could protest.

Outside, Sanskriti's voice tightened. "I told you I didn't have money for this. That was for something else. I never asked for any makeover."

Rose cupped her face gently, her tone deceptively soft. "Don't worry, baby. Tu boli thi na — tujhe zyada paisa chahiye. Toh ye samajh… investment hai."

(You said you wanted to earn more. Think of this as an investment.)

She gave a playful wink. "Chal, tujhe kapde kharidwati hoon." (Come on, I'll buy you clothes.)

"No," Sanskriti said, stepping back. "I don't have money for that. I'm not coming anywhere."

Rose's smile turned cold. "I'll pay for the clothes. Just come."

They walked into a lavish boutique where golden light shimmered off silk fabrics. The air smelled of perfume and new fabric. Mannequins stood like silent queens draped in expensive dresses.

Rose held up a dress. "Try this. It'll suit you."

Sanskriti shook her head. "No, I've never worn anything like that. I won't."

"Before this, there were a lot of things you never did," Rose replied softly, but her eyes were sharp. "Chal… pehen le. Client ko accha lagega." (Come on, wear it. The client will like it.)

Reluctantly, Sanskriti obeyed. She tried on outfit after outfit — each one more unfamiliar, each one pulling her further from who she once was. Rose nodded approvingly every time, her smile widening with each transformation.

They picked out several dresses and sandals before heading out. Just then, Sanskriti's eyes caught a black saree displayed on a mannequin — simple, elegant, haunting.

Rose noticed. "You want it?"

"No," Sanskriti said quickly, shaking her head.

"At least try it."

Minutes later, she stepped out of the trial room wearing the black saree. For a moment, she didn't recognize the woman in the mirror. Her reflection looked strong, beautiful — but distant.

Her voice was barely a whisper. "I can't even remember the last time I looked this beautiful."

Rose smiled. “You were already a princess when I first saw you. Today, I just helped the princess wear the clothes she deserves.”

Sanskriti’s lips curved into a faint, bitter smile. “We’re no longer princesses in the world’s eyes, Rose. No matter how impeccable we look… people will only ever see our flaws.”

Later, they went to the hospital. This time, only Sanskriti was allowed inside the ICU for the visit.

The air was cold and quiet, filled with the soft hiss of oxygen. Aaryan lay on the bed—his small body swallowed by tubes and wires—his chest rising gently with each breath from the ventilator.

Sanskriti sat beside him, his eyes still closed. Her heart tightened as she reached for his hand. His fingers twitched—barely a flutter—before curling around hers. That small movement struck her harder than any words. Aaryan’s lips lifted in the faintest curve, a sleepy, instinctive smile, as if he recognised his mother’s touch even from the darkness he was moving through.

The memory flashed before her eyes — his eighth birthday, just before he was admitted to the hospital. He had dragged her through the park, laughing and shouting with pure joy, insisting that she swing him around in circles until they both collapsed onto the grass. Later, they had gone to watch the dinosaur movie he'd begged for, where he'd buried his face in her arm every time the T-Rex roared. Afterwards, Nayan had lifted him onto his shoulders, and together they went to his favorite Chinese restaurant for noodles and ice cream — a small, happy family of three that now felt almost surreal to her.

Tears welled in her eyes as she leaned closer, pressing a soft kiss to his forehead. "Everything will be fine, beta," she whispered. "Mumma's here. I'll do anything to get you out of this — I'll fight the whole world if I have to. And when you're better again, we'll go for noodles and ice cream... just like before."

Her voice wavered, but she smiled anyway.

From outside the glass wall, Rose stood watching silently — her expression unreadable, her eyes soft with something that almost looked like respect.

At the billing counter, Sanskriti took out a small bundle of notes from her purse and spoke softly.

"Ma'am… please accept this much. I know I was supposed to pay some pending amount of the operation, but this is all I have for today."

The woman behind the counter looked her up and down, her tone cold and clipped. "I've been adjusting your payments because of your situation," she said. "But that doesn't mean you can take advantage of it. You'll have to pay the full amount today."

Behind her, two nurses whispered in Marathi, their voices low but sharp enough to sting. "Are baagh," one said, "hyanchya sathi mi saline ani bakiche vastu dusrya patient chyakadeun manage karti… par baga hya madam la, party la jaanyasathi tayyar aahet."

("Look at her — I've been managing saline bottles and supplies from other patients just to help her, and now she's dressed up like she's going to a party.")

Rose overheard it. Her eyes darkened with anger. Without a word, she reached into her bag, pulled out a thick bundle of □500 notes, and threw it on the counter.

"You want money?" she snapped. "Here. Take your damn money."

The notes scattered across the floor. The sound echoed through the quiet hallway. Rose turned sharply and walked out, her heels clicking hard against the tile.

"I'm sorry, madam," Sanskriti stammered, bending down to gather the fallen notes with trembling hands. "I'm so sorry…"

When she finally stood up, her eyes glistened with shame. "Please," she said softly to the billing clerk, "take whatever is required till tomorrow. You can return the rest later."

After settling the amount, she stepped outside. Rose was waiting near the gate, a cigarette between her fingers, arms crossed, still fuming. Sanskriti approached her gently.

"They've been helping me since the beginning," she said in a low voice. "Please ignore what they said. They don't know anything about us."

She glanced at the glowing tip of Rose's cigarette, then reached out, plucked it from her lips, and crushed it under her heel.

"Not here," she said softly. "At least not outside the hospital."

After a long night and attending multiple clients, Mallika came home with □80,000 in her purse. Rose dropped her at the gate and drove off.

Sanskriti slid the latch, stepped in, and found Nayan on the bed—awake, sober.

His eyes found her, gazing at her from head to toe.

For the first time in many nights, there was no smell of alcohol. Relief brushed her face and vanished.

She went straight to the bathroom, dropped her clothes into the bucket for later, and stood under a quick, cold shower. When she came out, his eyes were still on her.

"You didn't sleep?" she asked quietly.

"How can I," he said, his voice flat, "when you were out enjoying?"

The words struck her like a slap—not because of what he said, but because he said it sober. There was nothing left to blame it on.

Anger and fear twisted inside her, but beneath them she felt something else too—his hurt, his humiliation. She didn't answer. She simply turned away, lay on the bed while Nayan sleeping on the floor, and closed her eyes. The silence that followed was sharper than any fight.

The next morning, Sanskriti met Rose in her car. This time, Rose pressed a thick bundle of cash into her hands.

"Yeh le—hospital ke liye," she said softly. "Tere bacche ke liye hai."

(Take this—for the hospital. For your child.)

Sanskriti didn't speak. She only nodded and held the money tightly, as if afraid it might disappear.

A moment later, she said quietly, "Rose… I want to take a few days off."

Rose frowned. "Why? Is everything alright?"

Sanskriti only nodded again, avoiding her eyes.

"Is everything good between you and Nayan?" Rose asked gently.

Sanskriti turned away. “I… don’t want to talk about it right now. But I’ll be back soon.”

Rose exhaled, her tone softening. “As you feel comfortable, baby. Take your time. Just remember—we’ll have to make up for the leaves later.

She paused, studying Sanskriti’s face. “And if there’s anything you need to share… I’m right here.”

“Can I ask you something?” Sanskriti said softly.

“Yes?” Rose replied, a doubtful look flickering across her eyes.

“Why are you helping me so much?”

Rose exhaled, her voice gentle.

“Baby, koi apni ye line mein khushi se thodi aata hai. Majburi samajh sakti hoon… isliye jitna kar pati hoon, utna kar leti hoon tere liye.”

(Baby, no one enters in this line out of happiness. I understand helplessness… that’s why I do whatever little I can for you.)

“And what was your compulsion?”

Rose didn't answer immediately. Instead, she opened the car door for her and gave a faint, affectionate smile. "The day you're able to share your problems… maybe that day I'll tell you mine. Right now, what you're carrying is bigger. So go to the hospital, baby—and take care of the child."

At the hospital, she paid for the upcoming periodic vials and deposited an advance for the further procedures and major treatments. For the first time in weeks, the weight on her chest loosened—just a little.

The doctor Das called her into the cabin with a gentle smile.

"Sanskriti," he said, "a new drug has just been approved in India. It's shown remarkable results in cases like your son's. It could help him recover faster."

Her eyes filled instantly. She folded her hands, whispering, "Thank you." It wasn't only gratitude—it was relief, the kind that shakes loose after too many hopeless days. For the first time in so long, she allowed herself to believe that maybe, just maybe, things could change.

✧ ✦ ✧

A few days later, after she returned to work, everything shifted again. To cover up, Rose made her work the entire night—one client after another—until her body felt like it no longer belonged to her. When she finally returned home, the sky had turned a pale, sleepy blue. It was 7:30 a.m. Her legs felt unsteady beneath her, her eyes burned, but she kept walking.

As she climbed the stairs, a small voice broke through the still morning.

"Aunty! Where is Aaryan?"

It was Himanshu—the little boy from the neighborhood—his face bright with innocence.

Before she could answer, his mother appeared at the doorway. Her gaze moved from Sanskriti to her son, sharp and full of warning. She grabbed Himanshu's wrist and pulled him close.

"From now on," she said firmly, "you won't talk to that aunty. She's a dirty worker."

Then the door slammed shut.

The words didn't whisper—they sliced through the air, loud and final.

Sanskriti stood still, her breath caught somewhere in her throat. She didn't knock, didn't fight. What could she have said? The stillness around her felt deeper than the insult itself.

She walked back to her room, turned the key in the lock, and closed the door gently behind her.

Still in the same clothes, still carrying the smell of the night she'd endured, she sank onto the bed. Her eyes stayed fixed on the ceiling—empty, distant. No tears came this time. Only a heavy stillness, and the night replaying over and over inside her head.

It was nearly ten in the morning when the door creaked open. Nayan stumbled in, the smell of alcohol arriving before he did. His eyes were dull, his shirt untucked, his words already slurring.

"Where were you?" he demanded. "I was trying to find you all night."

Sanskriti looked up from the bed, her face pale with fatigue. "At least you could have called," she said quietly.

"My phone was switched off," he muttered, rubbing his forehead.

"So you were searching for me after getting drunk?" Her voice trembled, half anger, half disbelief. "Why are you always out all night, Nayan? What are you even looking for?"

He let out a dry laugh. "Toh kya karoon? Ghar baithkar yeh sochun ki tum wahan apni bhook mita rahi hogi?"

(What should I do? Sit at home imagining you're out there feeding your desires?)

The words hit her like stones. Without thinking, Sanskriti's hand rose and struck his face. Her eyes glistened as she choked out, "Main apne liye nahi jaati wahan, Nayan. Samjho yeh baat." (I don't go there for myself, Nayan. Understand that.)

For a heartbeat, the room froze in silence. Then, suddenly, his hand came up too—hard and fast. The slap landed sharp across her cheek.

Sanskriti stood frozen, staring at him in disbelief. In all their years together, he had never hit her. Something inside her cracked—quietly, like glass breaking in another room.

Too weak to argue, too tired to fight a drunk man's rage, she turned away. She walked to the bed, pulled the blanket over herself, and curled up tightly beneath it. Her shoulders shook as silent sobs escaped into the fabric.

Under the blanket, she felt utterly alone—fighting a three sided war. One battle for her son, clinging to life in a hospital. Another with her husband, who had promised to stand beside her but instead became another wound. And the third—with the world itself, cruel and unforgiving, waiting outside her door.

She closed her eyes and wished, just for a moment, that silence could erase everything.

Sanskriti woke around one in the afternoon. Her body felt heavy, her eyes swollen from crying. She moved slowly—washed her face, prepared a simple meal, ate in silence, and then packed her small cloth bag for the hospital.

Before leaving, she placed a folded note on the table beside Nayan's pillow.

You promised me you wouldn't drink. But every day, you've been breaking that promise—just like the promise you made to stand by me. Now I am all alone, unable to go back, afraid of what lies ahead.

I never imagined you would raise your hand on me, Nayan. That's the one thing I never expected from you.

Things are slipping out of our hands. Remember, this child is not just mine to fight for. He is ours.

I hope you remember that.

At the hospital, Sanskriti met Doctor Das near the ICU.

"How is Aaryan today?" she asked, her voice soft but steady.

"He's doing better than before," Das replied. "As I mentioned earlier, the new drug has arrived. We'll begin tomorrow after we run a few tests. But remember, Sanskriti… these are experimental drugs. Recovery isn't guaranteed."

"I understand, doctor," she said, nodding. "But something is better than nothing. At least we still have a chance."

Das smiled faintly. "Indeed. It's the only option left to us now." He paused, hesitating. "May I ask you something?"

"Of course," she said.

"It's none of my business," he continued gently, "but how are you managing the expenses? You know how costly this treatment is. And the drugs we're importing from the U.S.—even the shipping alone will cost nearly half a lakh."

Sanskriti was silent for a moment. Then she said quietly, "I don't even know how it's happening anymore, Doctor. Some distant relatives have been helping… but I don't know how long that will last."

"That's very kind of them," he said. "I also reached out to a few old contacts who helped with your bills earlier. If that blacklisted issue hadn't happened, we might've collected more funds."

She nodded, eyes distant. "Every night, I wonder—why us? Why only us? But now I've stopped asking. I just… take it one moment at a time."

Das smiled kindly. "I must say, Sanskritiji, you're a strong woman."

She returned a faint smile, eyes glistening.

A young junior doctor, who had been listening nearby, stepped closer. "Ma'am… may I tell you something?"

"Yes?" Sanskriti turned to her.

The young woman hesitated. "Three days ago, your husband came here to visit Aaryan."

Sanskriti frowned. “So?”

“He was drunk,” the doctor said softly. “Couldn’t even walk straight. I told him he wasn’t allowed to enter the ICU in that condition, and he… reacted badly.”

Sanskriti’s face went pale. “I’m sorry,” she said, her voice breaking. “I’ll make sure it never happens again.”

The two doctors exchanged a quiet look—one of pity, one of helpless understanding—before returning to their rounds.

Sanskriti stayed at the hospital that day. She didn’t want to go home. The thought of walking back into that house, facing Nayan again, felt unbearable.

Two hours later, Nayan appeared in the corridor—this time sober. He spotted her sitting alone on the bench outside the ICU and approached slowly.

“Did you read my letter?” she asked, without looking at him.

“Yes,” he said quietly. “I felt awful. I’m sorry for everything… for what I’ve been putting you through.”

"Sorry isn't enough every time, Nayan," she said, her tone calm but firm. "You need to face what's happening. You can't drown yourself in alcohol and expect things to fix themselves. You can't keep running from it."

Nayan buried his face in his hands, tears seeping through his fingers.

"I know I've ruined everything," he whispered. "I failed as a father first, and now as a husband… and as a man." His breath hitched. "Every time I think of it, I can only ask—why us, God? Why us?"

"You think I don't ask the same thing?" Sanskriti said, her voice trembling. "You're not the only one who's scared, Nayan. I'm scared too. But have you seen me drinking? Have you seen me lashing out at the only person trying to hold everything together? I've put away my shame, my dignity, my peace — all for our son. And you… you fight the one person who's still fighting for you."

She took a shaky breath. "Every time you say sorry, but then you do the same thing again. Even worse."

Her eyes filled as she wiped her tears with the back of her hand. “I can’t do this alone anymore, Nayan. I need your help.”

He lowered his hands slowly. She looked at him—tired, but honest.

“What you did yesterday,” she continued, “I can’t forget it. And because of that… I’ve decided I won’t continue this work anymore. You need to find another way. Especially now—these new drugs will cost even more. We’ll need to figure something out together.”

Nayan had no words. He covered his face again and broke down, sobbing quietly.

Sanskriti reached out and took his hand, tightening her grip. Nayan leaned forward, resting his head on her shoulder. She held him gently, one hand on his back, the other on his trembling arm.

His rough, untrimmed beard brushed against her neck as he cried. She didn’t move away. For the first time in a long while, they both allowed themselves to hold on—to find warmth, however faint, in each other’s grief.

In that sterile hospital corridor, amid the low hum of machines and the distant beep of monitors, they sat together—two broken souls, bound not by blame or anger anymore, but by the simple, desperate need for support in a world that had given them none.

By the time they left the hospital, the sun was low and the day moved at its own slow, silent pace. Sanskriti's phone buzzed again and again—ten missed calls, all from Rose. She didn't answer any.

Nayan noticed the screen lighting up and frowned. "Why aren't you picking up?" he asked.

"Let it ring," Sanskriti said softly. "I told you—I don't want to continue doing all this anymore."

"I know, love," Nayan said, his voice tired. "But at least tell her that."

"I don't have the strength to explain anything right now," she murmured. "And today was supposed to be a big client. If I answer, she won't leave me alone."

Nayan fell silent. A small part of him felt relieved—grateful that she was done with it. But another part, the one haunted by the thought of hospital bills and new drug costs, churned restlessly. His face showed both—the comfort and the quiet panic.

The evening stretched without a word between them. Around eight, a sharp knock broke the stillness.

Sanskriti froze, glancing at the door. The knocks came again, firmer this time. She gave Nayan a wary look; he returned it with the same unease.

He went to open the door.

Standing there, framed by the corridor light, was Rose—dressed in the same sequined outfit she wore for her nights out. Her eyes widened the moment she saw Sanskriti inside.

"Where the hell were you, Mallika?" she demanded, hands lifted in exasperation.

Nayan stepped aside as Sanskriti hurried forward.

"Why did you come here, Rose? That too dressed like this?"

"What do you want me to do, Mallika?" Rose shot back. "I already took the client's advance. What are you doing?"

Sanskriti glanced around nervously and lowered her voice. "Shh… come inside." She pulled Rose in and closed the door.

"What client?" she asked sharply. "Tell him I'm not working anymore."

Rose let out a short, incredulous laugh. "Do you even hear yourself? You think you can just say no? This isn't some random street client, Mallika. You can't just cancel on them."

"Then tell them my mood spoiled. Their mood can spoil too—I don't care."

"Your mood?" Rose stepped closer. "Do you even know who this client is? You said you wanted more money, remember? You said you wanted better places, not the dirty lanes. I worked my contacts to bring this deal to you. You're not walking away now."

"I'm not going," Sanskriti said firmly. "Tell them I met with an accident. Tell them anything."

Rose let out a bitter laugh. "And then what? You think clients like this just forgive and forget? Once you cross a line in this business, you can't erase it. You think I'll lie for you? Fine, I'll tell them whatever you want. But then tell me—how will you pay for your son's next treatment?"

"Here, you have to be professional to earn money, and you have to respect the contacts you work

with. Apna chalāyegī to dikhegī gutter ke bāju mein—hazaar, do hazaar mein bikti hui. Chalegā tujhe?
(If you try to act on your own, you'll end up by the gutter—sold for a thousand or two. Will that be okay for you?) Will you be able to cover your child's expenses with that?"

Her voice hardened as she turned toward Nayan. "Will you be able to pay? Do you have the money? You know, right—new drugs mean more expenses. Half a lakh just for shipment. You think pity will cover that?"

Rose looked back at Sanskriti. "If your son dies, do you know what happens next? Your husband's drinking gets worse. His anger will eat you alive. You've already lost one part of yourself, Mallika—don't lose another."

The room went dead quiet. Nayan's lips moved but no words came out. He didn't deny a thing.

Sanskriti felt trapped between the two—her child's fragile heartbeat on one side, her own emotional breakdown on the other.

Rose's tone softened slightly, almost like an older sister's. "Listen, once the cloth is stained, it doesn't stop spreading if you leave it. Better face it than let it swallow you. Come, Mallika. Get ready."

No one dared to argue anymore. Not Nayan. Not Sanskriti.

After a long silence, Sanskriti nodded faintly. She took the saree bag from Rose — the one she'd bought for this big client — her hands trembling as she unwrapped it.

Rose watched for a moment, then handed her a small lipstick tube.

"Here," she said quietly. "For later."

Sanskriti slipped it into her purse without a word, draped her saree, and pulled the pallu over her deep-neck blouse. The silence between her and Nayan was unbearable — too heavy to break. She looked at him only once before stepping out with Rose.

Downstairs, the air smelled faintly of gunpowder and firecrackers.

At a distance, in the society's shared ground, a group of boys in their late teens and twenties, along with a few men from the colony in their thirties, were lighting sparklers. Their laughter echoed through the night.

As Sanskriti and Rose walked toward the gate, one of them called out, loud enough for everyone to hear: “Where are you going, huh? Off somewhere with the Lal Gulab?”

Sanskriti stiffened. Her blood turned cold. They knew Rose’s name.

Another voice followed, younger, bolder—barely out of his teens.

“Arre Mallika! Ek baar humein bhi chance de do!”

(Hey Mallika, give us a chance too!)

Her heart sank. The world she’d tried to hide was now standing at her doorstep. She kept walking, head down, ignoring them.

Inside the cab, she finally turned to Rose. “How do they even know you? How do they know my name?”

Rose gave a faint, crooked smile. “It’s a small world, baby. They say you’re six steps away from anyone on this planet. In our world, it's four—sometimes three."

Mallika stared out of the window, her reflection trembling in the glass.

Rose continued, lighting a cigarette. "Everyone's got a dark side, sweetheart. Most are just too scared to show it. But here, we see it all. We live it."

Sanskriti's voice was low, bitter. "That boy couldn't have been more than eighteen. Who told him to talk like that?"

Rose exhaled a slow puff of smoke. "Here, even a whisper finds ten ears to hear it. You'll have to grow a thick skin, Mallika — it's the only way to survive. These comments won't stop; they'll only grow louder. And slowly, you'll see what humanity really looks like when the lights go out."

Sanskriti turned her face away, watching the city lights blur past the window. Somewhere deep inside, she wondered how far she'd already traveled from the person she used to be—and whether the road back even existed anymore.

As Mallika adjusted her saree and gathered her things to leave from client site, the client leaned back on the couch, a glass of half-finished whiskey in his hand. His voice broke the quiet of the room.

"Arre Mallika," he said lazily, exhaling smoke, "apne pati ko samjha zara. Hamare bar mein har waqt drama karta rehta hai."

("Hey, Mallika," he said lazily, exhaling smoke, "tell your husband to calm down. He keeps creating drama at my bar all the time.")

She turned toward him, her brows furrowing. "Mere pati? Aapke bar mein?"

("My husband? At your bar?")

He chuckled, swirling the glass. "Haan, wahi tera pati—kya naam tha uska? Nayan?

("Yeah, your husband — what was his name? Nayan?)

Last night he picked a fight with a police constable at my checkpoint bar. If a case had been filed, the bar might've been shut down. Explain things to him a little," he added, blowing a careless kiss into the air.

Mallika's voice trembled. "But how did you know… that he's my husband?"

The man grinned, leaning forward. "World is small, girl… very small."

He stubbed out his cigarette and buttoned his shirt. "Mujhe bhi aaj hi pata chala. Tujhse milne se pehle mere phantar log sab kuch brief karte hain—poori file hoti hai ladkiyon ki. Aur lafda bhi tere hi naam se hua tha."

("I only found out today. Before meeting you, my men brief me on everything — there's a complete file on every girl. And listen… that whole mess that happened? It was under your name.")

Mallika froze, her pulse quickening. "Mere naam se?"

He laughed softly, stepping closer. "Yeah, baby — under your name. But don't you worry, Mallika baby… we're not going to spare that constable this time."

He straightened his cufflinks, the arrogance in his voice curling like smoke. "And after meeting you… I feel like I could shut down all my businesses for you. What's one bar, anyway?"

In the cab, Mallika sat in silence, her mind spinning. The city outside slept restlessly — streetlights flickered, buildings slouched in darkness, and the night air carried the faint scent of rain and exhaust.

Beside her, Rose scrolled through her phone, the glow lighting up her sharp, tired features. “Oye,” she said after a while, glancing up, “us mote chutiya ka kuch dimag mein mat rakh. Bakwaas karna uski aadat hai.”

(“don’t let that fat asshole get in your head. Running his mouth is just what he does.”)

Mallika said nothing. Her fingers twisted the edge of her pallu again and again, knuckles pale in the dim light.

Rose sighed, shaking her head. “Aur tera pati… har jagah kaise pahunch jaata hai re? Samjha use zara. Shanti se dhanda karne de. Kitna piyega yeh aadmi? Kitna marega khud ko?”

(“And your husband… how does he manage to show up everywhere, huh? Talk some sense into him. Let you work in peace. How much will this man drink? How long will he keep destroying himself?”)

Mallika’s eyes remained fixed on the road ahead, expression blank. She wasn’t sure if she was angry, sad, or just numb.

The cab slowed as it entered her lane, the headlights gliding over cracked walls and half-asleep doorways. The digital clock on the dashboard blinked 3:02 a.m.

Rose leaned forward and pushed the cab door open for her. "Come on, get out," she said softly, her tone gentler than usual. "Get some rest. We'll meet tomorrow."

Mallika opened the door and stepped into the damp air. The building loomed before her — quiet, lifeless, its windows shut like tired eyes.

The taxi's taillights faded into the distance, leaving her alone under the flickering yellow streetlamp. For a moment, she just stood there, staring at her reflection in a puddle at her feet — blurred, broken by ripples.

Somewhere far off, a dog barked, and the faint rumble of a passing train drifted through the silence.

She adjusted her pallu, took a deep breath, and began climbing the stairs.

✧ ✦ ✧

When Sanskriti opened the door to her home, the stillness inside felt thick. The room was empty. Nayan wasn't there.

She changed quietly, folding her saree neatly on the chair, and was just about to lie down when a knock startled her. It wasn't the usual knock — slow, uneven, almost impatient, a rhythm she had never heard before.

Her heart jumped. She hesitated, then fastened the chain latch and opened the door just a crack.

Outside stood a man in his fifties with a curved nose and half-drunk eyes—Tatya, a neighbor and drinking companion of Nayan's. He had one arm hooked around Nayan's shoulder, struggling to keep him upright.

"Tai," he slurred, his tongue heavy, "Nayan saheb out zhalet… tyanna zopavtat ka att?" ("Sister, Nayan sir is completely out… can we lay him down?")

Sanskriti quickly unhooked the chain and opened the door. She grabbed Nayan by the arm, guiding his limp body to the bed. The moment she did, a sharp, foul smell hit her.

Her nose wrinkled—the stench of alcohol and urine was thick in the air. His pants were drenched and yellowed. As she dropped him onto the bed and tried to straighten his legs, her breath caught; there was more. A darker stain at the bottom—filth. He had lost control of everything, even his body.

Then she looked up at Tatya. "Wait outside," she said quietly, pointing toward the passage.

When she stepped out a moment later, her face was cold but steady. "Why is he so drunk again, Tatya? What happened this time?"

Tatya hiccupped before speaking. "Vahini, kai dada aikatach nahi… ajj tar tyanni sagli limitach paar keli pinyachi."

(Sister-in-law, he doesn't listen at all… today he crossed every limit.)

"Usse samjhaate nahi ho tum log?" Sanskriti snapped. "Kya samajhte ho tum sab milke?"

("Why don't you people talk some sense into him?)

Tatya spread his hands helplessly. "Mi kai samjavu, vahini? Main hi toh pehla tha jinhone bola, 'Bas karo, chalo ghar chalte hain.'"

(What can I explain? I was the first one who told him—enough, let's go home.)

"Ha, paile aur aakhri bhi," she said bitterly. "Kyuki company dene ke liye aur koi nahi milta usko."
(Yes, first and last—because you're the only one left to drink with him.)

Sanskriti crossed her arms. "And tell me this—what exactly happened at the bar the day before yesterday?"

Tatya looked startled. "How did you know about that?"

Her eyes narrowed. "Talk."

He rubbed the back of his neck, nervous. "Chhod dijiye, vahini…" (Let it be, sister…)

"Speak, Tatya."

He sighed, defeated. "That night, I was with the constable who let Nayan go that day. Two of his friends were sitting at our table. Nayan sahab was at the one opposite us. The moment the constable saw him drinking English liquor, he said—'Those five hundred rupees in your pocket, they belong to our lead Officer.'"

Sanskriti's eyes widened. "Then what?"

"Nayan lost his temper," Tatya said, shaking his head. "He grabbed the constable by the collar — so much rage… I had to step in. I told them, 'Let him go, sir, he lives in my building. The man's going through a rough time.' Only then they backed off."

She stared at him. "And today, you were drinking with him again?"

Tatya shrugged. "Well, it all happened just last night. I was the one who got him out of that mess, so we've been drinking together since."

Sanskriti let out a short, bitter laugh. "Wow. Must be proud of yourself, huh?"

Tatya hesitated. "Vahini, can I say something? Don't take it the wrong way?"

She folded her arms tighter. "Say it."

"Vahini, Nayan saheb's been acting strange lately," he said cautiously. "He keeps asking me—what news is there, what are people saying about you? What's the talk in the market?"

A flush of shame spread across Sanskriti's face. "And what did you tell him?"

"What could I say?" Tatya sighed. "Just small talk—the same things I told that constable. A little here, a little there. Sometimes I even made things up… but never anything dirty, vahini, I swear."

He paused, his face clouding. "But I don't know what's going on in Nayan's head anymore. He just keeps asking, over and over—'What else have you heard? Tell me, what else have you heard?' he doesn't listen to reason. Says he can't sleep, so he drinks until he collapses."

Sanskriti stood silent for a moment, her eyes cold and distant. Then she stepped back inside, her hand gripping the door handle.

Before closing it, she joined her hands slightly in front of her chest. "Tatya," she said quietly, "stay away from Nayan for a while. Understand?"

Tatya nodded weakly. "Yes, vahini."

She shut the door. Inside, the room smelled of alcohol and damp cloth.

Sanskriti stood beside the bed, staring at her husband's still form — his mouth half-open, his breath heavy and sour.

She wanted to hate him, but all she felt was exhaustion — an ache too deep for anger.

A few days passed.

When Sanskriti visited the hospital this time, Aaryan was better. The machines still surrounded him, but his eyes were open—soft, fragile, alive.

She sat beside his bed, pulling the chair close. As her shadow fell across him, Aaryan turned his head slightly and smiled — a small, tired smile, but enough to make her world pause. For the first time in months, they both were looking at each other.

Sanskriti felt a wave of relief, as if all her sacrifices and struggles were finally paying off. Tears filled her eyes as she leaned forward, afraid to even blink, afraid he might fade away again. He mumbled something faintly, his dry lips barely moving. She held his hand, her fingers unsteady, and bent closer.

“Maa… you look beautiful,” he whispered.

Her heart melted. She smiled through her tears. “Yes, beta… and you too. You’ll be out of here soon. The doctors have started a new treatment, and once it works, you’ll be walking again.”

Aaryan squeezed her hand weakly, the faintest spark of energy in his fragile grip. "Where is Dadda, Maa?" he murmured.

She hesitated for a second, then smiled softly. "He's busy with work, beta. But I'll tell him to come soon, okay? He'll be so happy to see how strong you've become."

The nurse entered quietly, her voice gentle but firm. "Madam, visiting time is over. We'll have to ask you to leave now."

Sanskriti nodded, even as her heart resisted. She leaned forward, pressed a gentle kiss to Aaryan's forehead, and whispered, "You'll be well soon, my love. Maa's right here with you." Her voice trembled, but she smiled through her tears. "You're my clever boy, na beta… keep fighting. Soon, you'll be walking again."

Aaryan's eyelids fluttered; a faint, peaceful smile touched his lips. He seemed to feel secure, and a quiet determination rose within him to fight the illness.

As she walked out of the ICU, Sanskriti turned once more to look through the glass window. His face was pale as paper, yet the subtle spark of who he was—his soft, natural charisma—still lingered on him.

She didn't know then that the kiss she left on his forehead might be her last.

Later that day, Sanskriti followed Nayan to the bar. She had already skipped her appointments for the night, knowing something inside her wouldn't rest until she saw the truth for herself.

The bar was dimly lit, its cracked signboard flickering against the drizzle. Through a small window with rusted iron bars, she stood quietly, peering in—the chatter of the noisy bar dissolving as she focused only on their words.

Inside, she spotted Nayan sitting with Tatya — half-slouched, half-lost — two glasses already on the table, the third being poured.

"So…" Nayan said, his words slightly slurred but sharp with restlessness, "yesterday you were saying something about Rose. I forgot—where were we?"

The two men talked in fragments, their voices rising and falling with every pour. Each round only pulled Nayan deeper. He wasn't just listening — he was searching, clinging to stray pieces of gossip like they might explain his pain or justify another drink.

Was it protectiveness? Jealousy? Or guilt? Even Nayan didn't know anymore what storm was raging in his mind.

From the window, Sanskriti watched him — his shaking fingers, his eyes darting with agitation, his whole being unraveling. This wasn't the man she'd married. This was a man breaking apart, quietly and publicly, one glass at a time.

Tatya leaned in, mumbling, "You know, Rose's client is also the owner of this hotel."

Nayan's eyes sharpened. "Seriously? Who's the owner?"

Before Tatya could answer, the door creaked open. The havaldar — the same one with whom Nayan had a spat recently — walked in, flanked by two of his friends. Their laughter sliced through the smoky air as they swaggered to the next table, carrying with them the heavy scent of liquor and authority.

"Kay re, Tatya," the havaldar called out, "aaj daaru fukat tikde miltey ka? Table change kela ahes ."

(“What, Tatya — free drinks over there? You changed the tables”)

Tatya stammered, “Nahi dada, ha majhya society madla ahe. Mitra ahe aple.” (“No, sir, he’s from my society. My friend.”)

The havaldar smirked, then said louder, so the whole bar could hear, “Have you ever seen a birthmark shaped like a heart… right on someone’s heart?”

His friends burst into laughter.

Something in Nayan snapped. Before anyone could blink, he was on his feet, rage flooding through him. He swung a hard punch straight across the havaldar’s face. The man reeled backward, shocked — not from pain, but from disbelief that anyone would dare hit him.

“You hit a cop!” one of his friends shouted, rushing forward. “Police la martos tu?” (“You dare hit a police officer?”)

Tatya tried to hold Nayan back, but Nayan shoved him aside, eyes blazing.

The havaldar pressed a hand to his bleeding lip. “Sala madarchod,” he spat, “tya divshi locker madhech sadat thevla paije hota! Chor!”

(“Bastard,That day I should have kept you rotten in the jail! Thief!”)

And then — everything stopped.

Sanskriti had stepped inside.

The room fell silent as she entered — the chatter, the laughter, even the bar receptionist froze. A woman walking into a men’s bar was rare enough. But one like her — clean, composed, beautiful in her simplicity — she didn’t belong here.

She pushed through the crowd and caught Nayan’s arm, pulling him back. “Bas karo!” she shouted. “Enough!”

Seeing her, Nayan’s rage faltered. His fists dropped. Shame and shock flickered in his eyes.

But the havaldar sneered, wiping his mouth. “Kai re? Baiko cha chelya maar na atta mala. Haatat bangdya ghatlya ka? Bai tar ahes tu gharachi.”

(“What’s wrong now? Lost your courage?

Go on—hit me again. Or are those bangles on your hands weighing you down? You're already the woman of your house, after all.")

The crowd murmured. Nayan froze.

Before anyone could react, Sanskriti's hand flew. The slap cracked through the room like a whip.

"I called you Bhau!" she shouted, trembling with fury. "I gave you respect — and this is how you speak about me? Did you even think once before uttering my name like that?"

The bar fell completely silent.

The havaldar stood still, cheek red, pride burning. But beneath it, something shifted — guilt, realization. Slowly, he lowered his gaze. "I'm sorry, vahini," he said hoarsely. "It was my mistake."

As the tension dissolved, the bar manager came rushing out from behind the counter. "Enough! Everyone out!" he barked.

He grabbed the phone and called the Bar owner. After a few curt words, he turned to the havaldar. "Sahab's orders — from today, you're not allowed here again."

The havaldar's eyes widened. Even his friends looked stunned. A cop, banned from a bar? It was unthinkable.

"Chala, chala," one of them muttered. "Let's go. We'll deal with this later."

The havaldar glared one last time, muttering as he left, "Bagu ajj ha bar 11 nantar kassa chalu thevto."
("Let's see how this bar stays open after 11 tonight.")

The air stayed heavy even after they left. Sanskriti turned to Nayan, who stood like a statue — guilt and confusion carved across his face. Without a word, she grabbed his hand and pulled him toward the counter.

Reaching into his pocket, she drew out a few crumpled notes and placed □500 on the counter. "For the drinks," she said softly. "Is there any more to pay?"

The bar manager shook his head. "No, madam. Please… keep it. I can't take it from you."

She looked at him for a moment. Then she left the money anyway, pressing it firmly onto the counter. leading Nayan out of the bar.

When they returned home, the air between them was thick with everything left unsaid.

Nayan threw the door shut behind them. “What was that?” he demanded.

Sanskriti looked up, weary. “What?”

“Why didn’t the receptionist take the money from you?”

She pressed a hand to her forehead, exhaling hard. “We just got into a fight with a police person, Nayan. He insulted me in front of everyone, half the bar was watching, and this is what you’re worried about? Why didn’t the receptionist take the money?” Her voice cracked. “What’s happening to you?”

Nayan’s tone turned sharp, trembling with something darker. “You don’t know what’s happening, Sanskriti? Are you making fun of me now? I know you knew the owner of that bar… Mallika.”

The name struck her like a slap. Sanskriti stepped back, eyes wide. “What did you say?”

He took a step forward, his face flushed, his eyes bloodshot. “Tell me the truth! You were there to meet him, weren’t you? The bar owner—the one whose place I drink at! You went there to meet him! What are you now—his keep? His—"

Before he could finish, Sanskriti shoved him hard. He stumbled backward, catching the curtain that separated the hall from the kitchen, barely steadying himself.

She was trembling—part fury, part disbelief. "I was there for you, idiot!" she shouted. "I followed you to make sure you were safe, to see what you were doing, who you were becoming. You think I did this for myself?"

Nayan's eyes burned with confusion and rage, his chest heaving. "Don't lie to me, Sanskriti! Tell me the truth!"

Her voice broke into a scream. "Enough!" And before she realized it, her hand flew across his face—hard, sharp, releasing every ounce of anger and grief that had been buried for weeks.

The slap sent Nayan staggering backward. He hit the edge of the kitchen platform, breath ragged, his hand searching blindly until it closed around a handle.

The moment blurred—no thought, no pause, only blind fury.

He swung.

It was the handle of an iron pan, and the metal struck Sanskriti hard on the head. The sound of metal against flesh cut through the room, sharp and final.

Sanskriti's cry split the silence, then faded. She tried to steady herself, her vision spinning.

A single warm drop touched her hand. She blinked, dazed, her vision blurring as she glanced down. Another drop followed, then another—until the trickle became a thin red stream, curling around her wrist and blooming through the folds of her saree like a spreading flower.

Her world dimmed. The last thing she saw was Nayan standing before her, frozen, the pan still in his hand. Then everything went dark.

For a moment, there was nothing—no words, no sound. Only the faint hum of the ceiling fan and the soft, spreading pool of red on the kitchen floor.

✧ ✦ ✧

Eight Years Later

Himanshu, Aaryan's childhood friend and now a college student, jumped onto a crowded city bus—only to realize he didn't have his wallet. His hands patted every pocket—nothing. A flicker of panic rose in him. Then, from behind him, came a gentle voice. "It's alright, beta. I'll pay for you." A voice he hadn't heard in years—familiar yet softened by time.

He turned and blinked in surprise. Sanskriti stood there, a faint smile softening the lines of her face.

"Thank you so much, aunty," he said with relief.

When they got down at the next stop, he turned again. "Really, thank you."

Sanskriti smiled. "No worries, beta. You remind me of my son, Aaryan. This much I can surely do."

"Then please, let me do something in return," Himanshu offered.

"Not required, beta," she said. Then, after a pause, added softly, "But tomorrow is Aaryan's birthday. If you'd like, you can come over."

His face lit up. "Of course! At seven?"

"Yes. Seven it is."

The next evening, Himanshu arrived at her apartment. The faint smell of incense mixed with chocolate cake. On the wall hung a framed photograph—a younger Sanskriti holding a laughing little boy in her arms.

"This is such a beautiful photo," Himanshu said sincerely.

Sanskriti smiled at it, her eyes glistening.

"Haan na? It was taken exactly nine years ago — on Aaryan's eighth birthday, just before he was admitted to the hospital. He looks so cute here, doesn't he?"

"He does," Himanshu said softly. "And so do you."

For a brief moment something flickered in her, a forgotten warmth, but she brushed it aside and took the cake from the fridge.

As he looked again at the photograph, he asked quietly, “So… you all don’t live together anymore?”

Sanskriti’s voice dimmed. “No. Nayan—my husband—took Aaryan away during his treatment, when I was hospitalized… He never came back.”

Himanshu hesitated, “Then… at least Aaryan could’ve been here today.”

Her silence filled the room. The only sound was the ceiling fan’s low hum.

Finally, she whispered, “You don’t know?

he didn’t make it.”

Himanshu’s expression fell. “I’m so sorry, aunty. I didn’t know.”

She nodded faintly. “Everyone talked about why my husband left. No one cared to ask what happened to Aaryan after that.” Her gaze stayed fixed on the photograph, eyes glassy with the kind of pain that has no words.

Himanshu stepped closer and gently placed a hand on her back. “It’s okay… I’m here,” he said softly.

That was all it took. The tears she'd caged for years broke free. Sanskriti leaned against him, sobbing, her whole body trembling. For a fleeting moment it felt as though she were crying in her grown son's arms.

Then the moment shifted.

A faint pressure against her back—at first she ignored it, thinking it accidental. But the touch lingered, changed, became deliberate.

Her breath caught. Her body stiffened. Memories she'd buried deep clawed their way up again—memories of helplessness, of being reduced to silence.

She pushed him away, her voice shaking. "What are you doing!?"

Himanshu froze. Shock flickered across his face, but not shame—just a hollow disbelief, the kind that comes from arrogance.

Her anger surged. She shoved him again, harder this time, and slapped him across the face.

"Get out!" she shouted, pointing to the door.

Real fear flashed in his eyes now. Without another word, he stumbled out, the door banging shut behind him.

She slammed the door shut and leaned against it, her breath uneven. Her eyes burned—not just with tears, but with disbelief.

It wasn't only the act that broke her. It was who had done it. Someone she once saw as a child… someone she thought would never look at her like that.

Buried beneath so many emotions, she was suddenly hit by another wave—an unwanted rush that trapped her once again in the same emotional maze she thought she had escaped.

Days passed. Every time Sanskriti left the building, she would see Himanshu. He never met her eyes. His head would lower, his steps would slow, and sometimes he would even change his route to avoid crossing paths with her.

One evening, Sanskriti sat alone on a bench near the beach, staring blankly at the waves. The sky had turned a warm shade of gold, painted by a sun preparing to disappear below the horizon.

A little farther away, Himanshu was laughing with his friends. When they finally left, he waved goodbye and began walking home alone.

As fate would have it, his path led past the bench where Sanskriti sat. The moment he saw her, his shoulders stiffened, and his eyes dropped. He tried to walk past without looking.

But then he heard it — a soft voice calling his name.

He ignored it at first. Then it came again, steadier this time. He turned. Sanskriti was looking at him, motioning for him to come closer.

Himanshu hesitated, guilt written across his face. Slowly, he walked toward her and sat down.

“So,” Sanskriti said quietly but firmly, “how long are you planning to keep running away from me like this?”

He stayed silent, staring at the sand.

“Yes… say it,” she said, her tone softer now, almost mocking.

“I’m sorry,” he murmured. “I’m sorry for everything.”

"Better than expected," she replied dryly.

"I mean it," he said quickly. "I don't know what I was thinking… what came over me. I felt so awful afterward. I know you always saw me like your own child… and I don't know what went wrong with me. I'm really sorry, Sanskriti tai."

Sanskriti let out a shaky breath. "Do you remember? When you were four, you used to call me Sanskriti Aai."

Himanshu's throat tightened. "I'm sorry… Aai."

"I won't forget what happened," she said softly. "But maybe… I can try to forgive."

She paused, looking out at the restless sea. Her voice trembled but stayed steady. "I can understand, a little, what must've gone through your head. The whispers, the things people say, the age you're at… all of it shapes how one thinks."

He nodded, ashamed. "Yes. I've been thinking about it too—how I even allowed such thoughts. Toward a woman I once called Aai."

Sanskriti turned to him. "It's because of that, isn't it? The story?"

He looked uncertain. “Story?”

“Yes… my story. The one everyone’s heard.”

He didn’t answer, but silence spoke for him.

“I didn’t want to bring it up,” he said at last. “But yes. That’s what influenced me.”

He hesitated, then asked, “Can I ask you something?”

“Go ahead.”

“Is it all true? What people say…?”

Sanskriti’s lips curved in a faint, dry smile. “As in what?”

He couldn’t bring himself to say the word.

She said it for him. “Prostitute?”

The word hit him hard—not because he hadn’t heard it before, but because of how she said it: without shame, with quiet defiance.

“Even if I was,” she continued, “does that make me less of a person? Does it give anyone—any man, any boy I once saw as my own son—the right to touch me or think of me that way?”

Himanshu shook his head, his voice breaking. “No.”

“Then tell me,” she asked, her voice rising, “why would I choose something like that?”

He whispered, “I… I don’t know.”

“For enjoyment, haan? You think it was for fun?”

“No,” he said quickly, eyes glistening. “After that day… I can’t even think like that anymore.”

Sanskriti gave a small, bitter smile. “Exactly.”

She took a long breath, her words trembling. “You remember Aaryan, right? The boy in that photo?”

“Yes,” he whispered.

“Then did it ever cross your mind,” she said, looking straight at him, “that Sanskriti aunty might have done all that—for money? For him?”

Himanshu lowered his gaze. “I thought… maybe you had been doing it from before.” His voice was barely audible. “I’m sorry,” he added, bowing his head.

Sanskriti took a slow breath before she spoke.

“He was admitted to the hospital because of a genetic condition that caused progressive muscle wasting — it’s called Duchenne Muscular Dystrophy.

“The first symptoms appeared right here, on this beach—Aaryan was only six. We were walking together when he suddenly fell, his body refusing to move. I thought it was just weakness. But then it kept happening.”

“We visited the doctor. They ran tests and said it was probably due to vitamin deficiency. We followed every treatment they suggested, but instead of improving, he grew worse.

“We went to another doctor, and this time they diagnosed him with something else entirely. Even that treatment was expensive.

“So we reached out to several NGOs. One of them agreed to help; they supported children with that specific disease. We thought we were lucky. But a few months later, a case came into the public eye — false claims by families from that same hospital, using fake diagnoses to get money from NGOs and government funds.

When they re-tested all the children, Aaryan's results came back negative — because he never had that disease in the first place. And so we were blacklisted.

"Once you're blacklisted by one NGO, the others won't touch you either. I can still remember that day — the shame, the helplessness. On one side, we'd lost all outside help. On the other, we still didn't even know what was truly wrong with our child.

"Later, after borrowing money and running more tests, we finally found the answer. Duchenne Muscular Dystrophy. Incurable. The only thing we could do was spend — endlessly — to keep him alive and comfortable.

"We went to government hospitals, but none offered treatment. Finally, we found a charitable trust that treated rare diseases at half the usual cost. But even half was too much for us.

"We sold my jewelry. Emptied our savings. Nayan worked extra shifts. But the bills never stopped coming."

She paused, her gaze fixed on the horizon. The sea glimmered like glass, endless and uncaring.

"One evening, while I sat waiting for the bus, a man offered me fifty thousand rupees for a night."

Himanshu's eyes widened.

"I tried to forget it," Sanskriti said quietly. "But the demand for money kept growing. Aaryan's pain was unbearable. We were desperate.

"Nayan and I talked for days. We cried. We argued. And in the end… we agreed. We told ourselves it would be temporary — just until things got better."

Her voice wavered but didn't break.

"The money helped, at first. But soon, Nayan began to change. He couldn't bear what we were doing, even though he had agreed. He stopped eating. Started drinking.

"And then… he started hitting me. Calling me names. Making me feel filthy. He forgot about our son — the reason we'd done it all in the first place.

"By then it was too late to turn back. I was standing on a thin edge — one step in any direction and I would fall. So I chose to fall… if it meant saving my son.

"Aaryan was my only purpose. My only hope. I just wanted to bring him home, healthy."

Her eyes grew distant. "But fate kept turning its pages."

"One night, after another fight, Nayan hit me on the head with a pan. I lost consciousness. He took me to the hospital. I was in a coma.

"While I lay unconscious, the money stopped. Aaryan's treatment was cut off. Nayan moved him to a government hospital near his hometown — a place with no facilities for his condition.

"He lost his young life there. And Nayan disappeared."

Himanshu's eyes filled. Sanskriti continued, her tone almost numb.

"When I woke up two months later, there was no one left. Rose and my flat owner — a distant relative named Megha — were the only ones who came to help me. I didn't even know where I was, or what had happened to my family."

"Eventually, I learned that Nayan had taken Aaryan away. When I reached out to the hospital to ask about him… and they told me he had passed away ten days earlier."

"It felt as though my child had given me life by surrendering his own."

Her voice trembled. "When I heard the news, it was as if my soul had slipped out of me. My child was gone… and I wasn't even there to say goodbye."

"All I could do was accept what life had become and be grateful that I still had a roof over my head. Acceptance was all that was left for me."

She looked down, her fingers trembling slightly.

"I cried for days, for nights that had no end. Cried for my child, for my marriage, for the path I chose that led nowhere, for the dignity I lost, and for everything that slipped away. Until one day, I promised myself… I wouldn't cry again."

"I even thought of ending it all. But I couldn't. Because I didn't want another woman, another mother, to go through what I had.

"So I joined three NGOs. Two that help children get medical treatment. And one that protects women from abuse — women like me.

“Whenever a child is saved now, I feel like I’ve saved a small part of Aaryan.”

Himanshu was sobbing, his shoulders trembling as tears streamed down his face. Sanskriti reached out, placed her hand gently on his head, and tousled his hair. Wiping her own tears, she managed a soft, reassuring smile

“I hope,” she said softly, “that from now on, I’ve given you a reason to be grateful every day — and the courage to begin your life with a fresh perspective.”

---- The End----

www.ingramcontent.com/pod-product-compliance
Ingram Content Group UK Ltd.
Pitfield, Milton Keynes, MK11 3LW, UK
UKHW041347190726
13845UKWH00026B/459

9 789355 920287